Bella and Rosie
Love Spring

BY MICHÈLE DUFRESNE

PIONEER VALLEY EDUCATIONAL PRESS, INC.

"Look," said Bella.

"Spring is here."

"I like spring!" said Rosie.

"Look," said Bella.

"I can see flowers."

"Look," said Rosie.

"I can see leaves."

"Look," said Bella.
"I can see birds
up in the tree."

"Look," said Bella.

"I can see mud!"

"I love spring," said Bella.

"Oh, dear," said Rosie.